Bad Zombie Movie

Level 6G

Written by Lucy George
Illustrated by Sernur Isik

What is synthetic phonics?

Synthetic phonics teaches children to recognise the sounds of letters and to blend (synthesise) them together to make whole words.

Understanding sound/letter relationships gives children the confidence and ability to read unfamiliar words, without having to rely on memory or guesswork; this helps them to progress towards independent reading.

Did you know? Spoken English uses more than 40 speech sounds. Each sound is called a *phoneme*. Some phonemes relate to a single letter (d-o-g) and others to combinations of letters (sh-ar-p). When a phoneme is written down it is called a *grapheme*. Teaching these sounds, matching them to their written form and sounding out words for reading is the basis of synthetic phonics.

Consultant

I love reading phonics has been created in consultation with language expert Abigail Steel. She has a background in teaching and teacher training and is a respected expert in the field of synthetic phonics. Abigail Steel is a regular contributor to educational publications. Her international education consultancy supports parents and teachers in the promotion of literacy skills.

Reading tips

This book focuses on three sounds made with the letters ie: igh as in tie, ee as in field and e as in friend.

Tricky words in this book

Any words in bold may have unusual spellings or are new and have not yet been introduced.

Tricky words in this book:

scene one two some their budgie four mixture action caught

Extra ways to have fun with this book

After the reader has read the story, ask them questions about what they have just read:

What did Zombie help the friends find?

Who is your favourite character, and why?

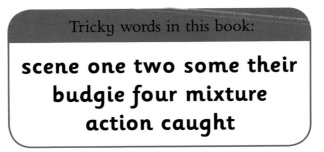

Freeze Zombie! You're under arrest! Ooo, hang on, let me just eat this doughnut first.

A pronunciation guide

This grid contains the sounds used in the stories in levels 4, 5 and 6 and a guide on how to say them. /**a**/ represents the sounds made, rather than the letters in a word.

/**ai**/ as in game	/**ai**/ as in play/they	/**ee**/ as in leaf/these	/**ee**/ as in he
/**igh**/ as in kite/light	/**igh**/ as in find/sky	/**oa**/ as in home	/**oa**/ as in snow
/**oa**/ as in cold	/**y+oo**/ as in cube/music/new	long /**oo**/ as in flute/crew/blue	/**oi**/ as in boy
/**er**/ as in bird/hurt	/**or**/ as in snore/oar/door	/**or**/ as in dawn/sauce/walk	/**e**/ as in head
/**e**/ as in said/any	/**ou**/ as in cow	/**u**/ as in touch	/**air**/ as in hare/bear/there
/**eer**/ as in deer/here/cashier	/**t**/ as in tripped/skipped	/**d**/ as in rained	/**j**/ as in gent/gin/gym
/**j**/ as in barge/hedge	/**s**/ as in cent/circus/cyst	/**s**/ as in prince	/**s**/ as in house
/**ch**/ as in itch/catch	/**w**/ as in white	/**h**/ as in who	/**r**/ as in write/rhino

Sounds this story focuses on
are highlighted in the grid.

/f/ as in phone	/f/ as in rough	/ul/ as in pencil/ hospital	/z/ as in fries/ cheese/breeze
/n/ as in knot/ gnome/engine	/m/ as in welcome /thumb/column	/g/ as in guitar/ghost	/zh/ as in vision/beige
/k/ as in chord	/k/ as in plaque/ bouquet	/nk/ as in uncle	/ks/ as in box/books/ ducks/cakes
/a/ and /o/ as in hat/what	/e/ and /ee/ as in bed/he	/i/ and /igh/ as in fin/find	/o/ and /oa/ as in hot/cold
/u/ and short /oo/ as in but/put	/ee/, /e/ and /ai/ as in eat/ bread/break	/igh/, /ee/ and /e/ as in tie/field/friend	/ou/ and /oa/ as in cow/blow
/ou/, /oa/ and /oo/ as in out/ shoulder/could	/i/ and /ai/ as in money/they	/c/ and /s/ as in cat/cent	/y/, /igh/ and /i/ as in yes/sky/myth
/g/ and /j/ as in got/giant	/ch/, /c/ and /sh/ as in chin/ school/chef	/er/, /air/ and /eer/ as in earth/bear/ears	/u/, /ou/ and /oa/ as in plough/dough

Be careful not to add an 'uh' sound to 's', 't', 'p',
'c', 'h', 'r', 'm', 'd', 'g', 'l', 'f' and 'b'. For example,
say 'fff' not 'fuh' and 'sss' not 'suh'.

The cast, crew and director are
gathered and ready to start
shooting the latest movie,
Bad Zombie Movie.
"Get in your places, everyone!"
shouts the director.

In **scene one**, Auntie is in a field struggling with her heifer.

"Attack now, Zombie!" shouts
the director.

Zombie lumbers into the field,
but instead of attacking, he
helps Auntie untie her heifer.

In scene **two**, the police are
waiting for a thief.

Zombie is meant to attack,
but instead he helps the police
catch the thief.

In scene three, **some** friends have lost **their budgie**.

Zombie is meant to attack,
but instead he helps the friends
find their budgie.

In scene **four**, a niece is baking cookies. Zombie is meant to attack, but instead he helps her stir the **mixture**.

"Zombie! You are meant to
be bad. You have one more
chance!" shouts the director,
getting very stressed. "**Action**!"

The police have **caught** the thief,
the friends have their budgie,
and Auntie and her niece are
sharing out cookies.

Zombie is meant to attack them
all, but instead he joins them for
a cup of tea.

"Cut!" cries the director.
"Good grief! This is beyond
belief! This movie is called
Bad Zombie Movie!

It's meant to have a bad
zombie in it! But instead,
it's just a bad movie!"
And with that he storms off.

OVER **48** TITLES IN SIX LEVELS
Abigail Steel recommends...

Some titles from Level 4

The Circus Mice
978-1-84898-582-7

Monster's Night
978-1-84898-583-4

The Mummy Code
978-1-84898-585-8

Some titles from Level 5

The Gigantic Bear
978-1-84898-586-5

Celebrity Celia
978-1-84898-587-2

The Cemetery Dance
978-1-84898-588-9

Other titles to enjoy from Level 6

Hugh is New
978 1 84898-590-2

Clumsy Eagle
978-1-84898-591-9

Owen the Astronaut
978-1-84898-593-3

An Hachette UK Company
www.hachette.co.uk

Copyright © Octopus Publishing Group Ltd 2012
First published in Great Britain in 2012 by TickTock, an imprint of Octopus Publishing Group Ltd,
Endeavour House, 189 Shaftesbury Avenue, London WC2H 8JY.
www.octopusbooks.co.uk

ISBN 978 1 84898 592 6

Printed and bound in China
10 9 8 7 6 5 4 3 2 1